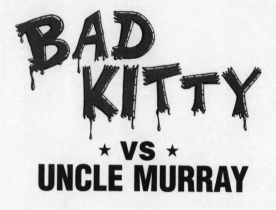

★ VS ★
UNCLE MURRAY

NICK BRUEL

BAD KITTY

★ VS ★

UNCLE MURRAY

THE UPROAR AT THE FRONT DOOR

SQUARE
FISH

ROARING BROOK PRESS
NEW YORK

SQUARE
FISH

An Imprint of Macmillan

Square Fish and the Square Fish logo are trademarks of Macmillian and are used by
Roaring Brook Press under license from Macmillian.

ISBN 978-0-312-67483-0
LCCN 2011280781

Originally published in the United States by Neal Porter Books,
an imprint of Roaring Brook Press
First Square Fish Edition: May 2011
Square Fish logo designed by Filomena Tuosto
mackids.com

7 9 10 8 6

AR: 2.9 / LEXILE: 620L

To Neal

• CONTENTS •

•CHAPTER ONE•

PUSSYCAT PARADISE

WELCOME, KITTY!

Welcome to Pussycat Paradise, where everything you see is made entirely out of **FOOD**—food for your belly!

The mountains are made out of kibble. The trees are made out of sausages and bacon. Cans of cat food grow out of the ground. And the grass is made out of catnip.

Yes, Kitty! Eat! EAT! Food is everywhere! The rocks are made out of turkey and giblets. The dirt is made out of tuna fish. Even the rivers flow with beef gravy.

And the best part, of course, is that YOU are the only one here! No dogs to hound you. No people to make you take a bath. There is no one else here. Only you.

Be careful, Kitty. Don't touch that can. It's the only thing holding up that gigantic chicken liver.

OH NO! TOO LATE! The gigantic chicken liver is going to fall! Look out, Kitty! LOOK OUT!!

WHOOPS!

Sorry, Kitty. I hope I didn't wake you when I dropped the suitcase.

That's right, Kitty. We're going on a little trip. We'll be gone for a while.

Sorry, Kitty. You're not going with us. You'll have to stay home with Puppy.

Oh, don't be like that, Kitty. We'll be back in just a week. And when we get back, we'll have a REALLY BIG SURPRISE for you!

That's right, Kitty. **A REALLY BIG SURPRISE!** You like surprises, don't you?

In the meantime, Kitty, you won't be alone. We found someone who's going to stay here and feed you and take good care of you and Puppy while we're gone.

In fact, that must be him!

Where did Kitty go? Oh, well. At least Puppy is excited to see who's here.

IT'S GOOD OL' UNCLE MURRAY!

There you are, Kitty. Don't you want to say "Hi" to good ol' Uncle Murray?

Awww! You're a good dog, aren't you?

UNCLE MURRAY'S FUN FACTS

I was just wondering about that.

WHY ARE SOME CATS AFRAID OF PEOPLE?

No one ever talks about a "scaredy-giraffe" or a "scaredy-penguin" or even a "scaredy-dog," but everyone's heard of "scaredy-cats"! That's because cats use fear as a very valuable tool for survival.

The average weight for a cat is only around 10 pounds. Imagine what your life would be like if you lived with someone who was almost TWENTY TIMES BIGGER than you! That's what life is like for a cat living with a human being. Having good reflexes to avoid being stepped on or sat upon is very important.

CAT: AROUND 10 POUNDS.

BIG, FAT, GOOFY-LOOKING AUTHOR OF THIS BOOK: 185 POUNDS.

REALLY? DOES THIS BOOK MAKE ME LOOK FAT?

But sometimes a cat's fear of people can become exaggerated. Sometimes this happens when a kitten is raised without any human contact. It can also happen if a cat or a kitten has had a bad experience with a person.

But I'm a nice guy! I wouldn't hurt a fly, much less a dog or a cat, no matter how goofy it is.

It doesn't matter. A cat's instinct always tells her to be careful around people, especially strangers. The best way to get a cat to grow used to you is to be patient, be gentle, be quiet, and try not to take the cat's reaction to you too personally.

And one more thing . . . Try not to make any sudden, loud noises. Cats hate that.

No loud, sudden noises. Got it! What kind of jerk do you think I am? Everybody knows that!

Bye, Uncle Murray! Thank you for taking care of Kitty and Puppy while we're gone. We'll see you in a week!

By the way, you have to really push hard on this door to close it. If you don't, it won't really shut properly.

— Okey doke! Goodbye! Good luck!

•CHAPTER TWO•
HIDE!

You know what, dog . . . I think the best thing to do right now is to sit down, relax, have some lunch, and maybe watch a little . . .

Lousy, rotten, goofy cat . . . goin' around pretending she's a pillow . . . freaking me out . . . made me spill my lunch . . . making a big mess . . . making me get a washcloth when all I really want to do is . . .

HOLY SALAMI! That goofy cat's just making things worse and worse!
ZANG

I see you there pretending to be a dishrag again, ya goofy cat! Don't scream at me. Don't scream at me. Don't scream at me. Don't scream at me. Don't scream at me. Don't scream at me . . .

49

All I really wanted was to sit down, relax, have some lunch, and maybe watch a little TV.

All I really wanted was to sit down, relax, have some lunch, and maybe watch a little TV.

All I really wanted was to sit down, relax, have some lunch, and maybe watch a little TV.

All I really wanted was to sit down, relax, have some lunch, and maybe watch a little TV.

•CHAPTER THREE•
THE KITTY DIARIES

FWING!

No FOOD. NO WATER.
MONSTER IS STILL
OUT THERE. IT HAS
BIG FEET.
DOG SMELLS BAD.

FIVE DAYS NOW. DOG STILL SMELLS BAD. DOG IS UGLY, TOO. DOG DROOLS A LOT. SO THIRSTY. MAYBE I COULD DRINK DROOL.... NO. I WOULD RATHER MONSTER EAT ME.

•CHAPTER FOUR•
UNCLE MURRAY STRIKES BACK

Y'know, . . . this
stuff doesn't
look half bad.

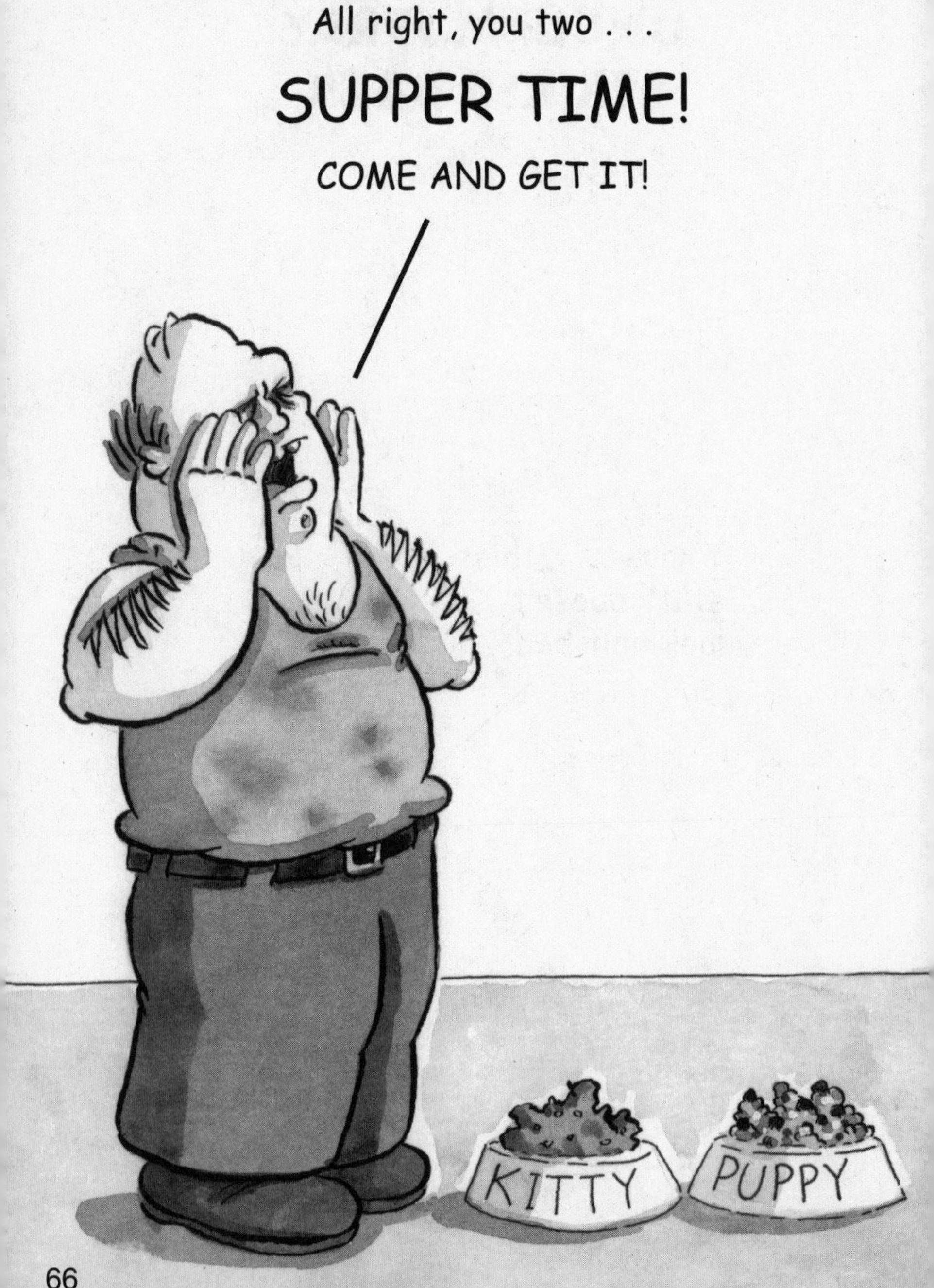
All right, you two . . .
SUPPER TIME!
COME AND GET IT!
KITTY
PUPPY

sigh
What's a nice dog like you doing with a goofy cat like that?
UPPY
KITTY

Oh, well . . . Let's go, dog. Why don't you help me clean this place up.

Y'know, dog . . . when I was just a kid, I had a pooch a lot like you. He was a good dog, too.

I named him Sam, and I found him lost and hungry in an alley near where I lived. He was all white except for some black spots on his face and one of his back legs.

Anyways, I still had half a sandwich on me from lunch so I tossed it to him. Boy, oh, boy was he happy to get some food into his little dog belly. You'd think he hadn't eaten anything in a year. It was just baloney, after all. No mustard, even.

I used my belt as a leash and put it around Sam's neck. At first I thought he'd go crazy when I started to pull him, but he didn't. In fact, he barked and licked my hand the whole way home.

But there was a problem. My mother wouldn't let me keep Sam in the house 'cause my baby sister was real allergic to dogs. I guess it was true, 'cause she still is. I told my mom I would keep Sam only in my room, but she told me that wouldn't really work. She was right.

So I did the only thing I could think of . . . I took little Sam to a dog shelter where they'd feed him and take good care of him.

They were real nice to Sam there. He had his own little cage, and there were lots of other dogs there for him to talk to. But the best part was that they said I could come visit him every day after school. So I did!

I went to visit Sam every single day, and each time he saw me he'd jump up and lick my face and wrestle me to the ground like he was sayin' "Gee, I'm really happy to see you! Where've you been?"

Each day, I taught him a new trick. I taught him to sit and to stay. I taught him to beg and to roll over. I even taught him geography. NAHHH! I'm just kidding about that last one. But he really was smart.

K-CHOO!

Gee, Sam and I had a lot of fun together. Then one day I walked in and didn't see him there.

A lady who worked at the shelter told me a family had come in just after I left the day before, fell in love with Sam, and took him home. She said they were real nice people and promised to feed him and take good care of him. But that didn't help. I started crying like Niagara Falls. He may not have lived with me, but Sam was <u>MY</u> <u>DOG</u>!

I thought for sure that I'd never see little Sam again.

But then, one day, about a year later, as I was walking through the park, I looked over and saw a little girl playing with a dog that looked a whole lot like my Sam. He was all white except for some black spots on his face and one of his back legs. It was him! And they were having a swell time. Sam was even doing some of the same tricks that I taught him.

It hurt me so much inside to see this little girl playing with my dog. MY DOG. But then I looked at how much fun they were having and how happy he looked, and I thought to myself . . . all I ever really wanted for that lost, hungry dog sitting alone in that alley was for someone to take him home and feed him and take good care of him. Right? And that's what I got.

I loved that dog, and now I knew that someone else loved that dog as much as me.

It was one of those days that was both real good and real bad at the same time.

81

UNCLE MURRAY'S FUN FACTS

WHY ARE CATS AFRAID OF VACUUM CLEANERS?

It's not the vacuum cleaner that frightens cats so much as the sudden, loud noise it makes. Most cats will react quickly to any sudden, loud noise like a car horn, or a firecracker, or someone yelling.

Cats can hear very, very well—even better than dogs. In fact, a cat can hear three times better than a human being. That's why a cat can hear a mouse rustling through the grass from 30 feet away. But it's also why loud noises are particularly painful for cats. And that's what inspires their fear.

RUSTLE

ZZZZZ...
DING!

Fear of loud noises is another survival tool for cats. If a little noise is a signal that something to eat might be nearby, then a very loud noise acts the same as a fire alarm held up next to their ears. And that means DANGER. And that means FIGHT or RUN AWAY.

When a cat is frightened, running away or hiding is a common response. But sometimes if a cat feels trapped or cornered, she'll stand still while unusual things happen to her body.

First, all of the fur on her body will stand on end. Then the cat will arch her back up using all sixty of her vertebrae—humans have only thirty-four, by the way. This will make the cat look much bigger; a tactic it uses to intimidate its enemies. But the sign to be very aware of is when a cat has turned its ears back. A cat will do this when it feels like fighting back and wants to protect those sensitive ears. That is a clear sign to back away from a VERY angry cat that could attack you.

DANGER

MORE DANGER

LOTS AND LOTS OF DANGER

Never mind all that ear stuff! I gotta go grab that cat!

•CHAPTER FIVE•
CATCH THAT KITTY

EEEEEEEEEECH

88   *Hark!

96

97

LOOK OUT FOR THE SPATULA!

WOW! THIS IS REALLY GOOD POPCORN!

98

•CHAPTER SIX•

KITTIES TO THE RESCUE

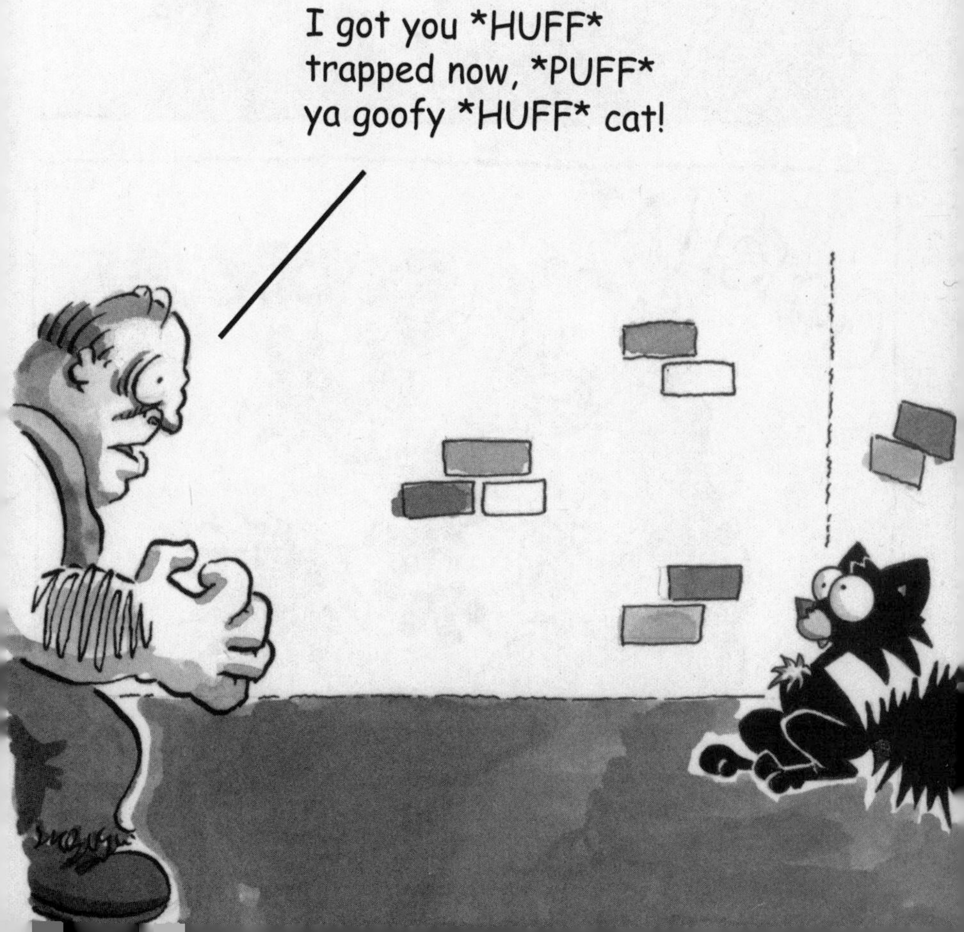

*Let us in, and I mean RIGHT MEOW!

121

NOOOOOOOOOO!
NOT YOU! You don't get to leave! Why? Because I'M the one that's leaving!

That's right! You heard me! As soon as I open this door, I'll be free. FREE! No more goofy cats screaming in my face and eating my shoes. No more biting and scratching and chasing me down the street. Outside this door is a big, wonderful world where goofy cats don't turn into furry whirlwinds that hit me on the head with a spatula. And soon I will be a part of that world once again!

YAWN

•CHAPTER SEVEN•
KITTY ON HER OWN

133

WHY ARE SOME CATS AFRAID OF BEING ALONE?

Cats are independent animals. There's no question about that. They're very good at taking care of themselves in the wild. But when cats have become house cats, they usually become "bonded" with their owner.

When a cat becomes very close, even dependent on a human being for food or protection, that's called "bonding."

MEOW?

And sometimes when that bond is broken, even for just a little while, some cats might exhibit "separation anxiety." Have you ever seen a baby begin to cry just because her Mommy has left the room for just a few seconds? That's a good example of "separation anxiety," and even cats can get it.

Leave cats alone for too long and they'll start to cry out to see if anyone is in the house, just like a baby. Sometimes they'll even lose their appetite and not

eat. The most anxious cats will even pull out clumps of their own fur because of nervousness.

The solution for all fears is to let the cat gradually grow used to whatever scares them. Cats can adapt very quickly.

If a cat is afraid of people, keep your distance and step a little closer day by day while also letting her come to you under her own power. If your cat is afraid of loud noises, try to keep the sound down at first if possible, and then increase the exposure a little bit each day.

And if the cat is afraid of being alone, give her time to adjust as she learns that you'll eventually return. She'll hate being alone at first, but in time she'll learn that there's nothing to be afraid of once you keep coming back.

I made a promise to feed you all week and take good care of you all week. And I'm going to keep that promise even if you act mean and goofy to me all week.

So, let's you and me make a deal, cat. We're going to be stuck together for the next few days. I'm going to feed you and take good care of you no matter what.

And in return . . . how about you be just a little nicer to me.

PURR.

Well, okay then.

That turned out to be easier than I thought.

Although . . . something tells me this is STILL going to be a very long week.

• EPILOGUE •

Thank you so much, Uncle Murray, for taking such good care of Kitty and Puppy. I know they can be a real handful. I hope they weren't too much trouble.

Fish.

What did you say, Uncle Murray?

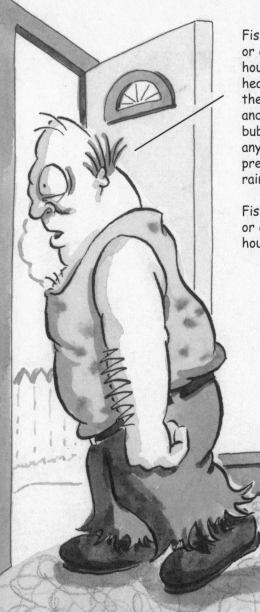

Fish don't bite or scream or chase you around the house or hit you on the head with a spatula. All they do is swim around and make nice little bubbles that don't hurt anybody. And they're pretty. Pretty like little rainbows. Fish.

Fish don't bite or scream or chase you around the house or . . .

Hmmm . . . Oh, well. Goodbye, Uncle Murray. And
thanks again.

HI, KITTY!
Did you miss us?

Awwwww! We missed you, too, Kitty!

HEY! Do you remember that REAL BIG SURPRISE we promised you? Do you? DO YOU?!

Well, here she is!

To be continued . . .

• APPENDIX •
A SELECTION OF PHOBIAS

A "phobia" is a strong fear of a specific object or a specific situation. Most of the time the fear is irrational, meaning that the person who has the phobia really has nothing to fear. For instance, a boy might be afraid of worms (Scoleciphobia), but that doesn't mean the boy has any real reason to be afraid of worms, other than he thinks they're scary and doesn't want them anywhere near him.

Ten percent of the people who live in the United States have a phobia. That's over thirty million people! This means that phobias are very common and nothing to be ashamed of.

We've seen a lot of different examples of fear in this book. The following is a small selection of the more than five hundred known phobias.

Agrizoophobia—Fear of wild animals.

Ailurophobia (also, Elurophobia)—Fear of cats.

Amychophobia—Fear of scratches or being scratched.

Cynophobia—Fear of dogs.

Ligyrophobia (also, Phonophobia)—Fear of loud noises, also, fear of voices or one's own voice.

Lilapsophobia—Fear of hurricanes or tornadoes.

Monophobia (also Autophobia)—Fear of being alone.

Olfactophobia (also, Osmophobia)—Fear of smells or odors.

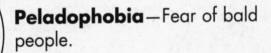

Peladophobia—Fear of bald people.

Phagophobia—Fear of swallowing, eating, or being eaten.

Pnigophobia—Fear of being choked or smothered.

Teratophobia—Fear of monsters.

• ABOUT THE AUTHOR •

NICK BRUEL has written and illustrated some pretty funny books, including *Poor Puppy, Boing, Bob and Otto, Little Red Bird,* and *Who is Melvin Bubble?,* winner of the North Carolina Children's Choice Award. HOWEVER, he is probably best known as the author of the Tennessee, Wyoming, and Indiana Children's Choice Award winner *Bad Kitty* (available in regular and special Cat-Nipped editions), about which some very important people said:

★"Perhaps the hammiest, most expressive feline ever captured in watercolors."
—*Kirkus Reviews*, starred review

★"Will have youngsters howling with laughter."
—*Publishers Weekly*, starred review

He is also infamous for his Bad Kitty chapter books, *Bad Kitty Gets a Bath* (winner of a 2009 Gryphon Honor), and *Happy Birthday, Bad Kitty*. Visit him online at www.nickbruel.com.

GO FISH

NICK BRUEL

What did you want to be when you grew up?
I tell this story all the time when I visit schools. When I was in first grade, there was nothing I liked to do more than to write stories and make little drawings to go with them. I thought the best job in the world was the one held by those people who had the comic strips in the newspapers. What better job is there than to wake up each morning and spend the day writing little stories and making little drawings to go along with them. So that's what I did. I wrote stories and I drew pictures to go along with them. And I still do that to this day.

When did you realize you wanted to be a writer?
I always liked to write stories. But it wasn't until high school when I spent a lot of time during summer vacations writing plays for my own amusement that I began to think this was something I could do as a career.

What's your first childhood memory?
Sitting in my high chair feeling outraged that my parents were eating steak and green beans while all I had was a bowl of indescribable mush.

SQUARE FISH

What's your most embarrassing childhood memory?
Crying my eyes out while curled up in my cubbyhole in first grade for reasons I can't remember. I didn't come back out until my mother came in to pick me up from school.

What's your favorite childhood memory?
Waking up early on Christmas morning to see what Santa brought me.

As a young person, who did you look up to most?
My father. He was a kind man with a great sense of humor.

What was your worst subject in school?
True story: In eighth grade, I was on the second string of the B-Team of middle school baseball. I was up at bat only twice the entire season. I struck out and was beaned. It was generally recognized that I was the worst player on the team. And since our team lost every single game it played that year, it was decided that I was probably the worst baseball player in all of New York State in 1978.

What was your best subject in school?
Art, with English coming in a close second.

What was your first job?
I spent most of the summer after my junior year in college as an arts and crafts director at a camp for kids with visual disabilities in Central Florida. I won't say any more, because I'm likely to write a book about it someday.

How did you celebrate publishing your first book?
I honestly don't remember. A lot was happening at that time. When *Boing!* came out, I was also preparing to get married. Plus, I was hard at work on *Bad Kitty*.

Where do you write your books?

As I write this, I'm the father of a one-year-old baby. Because of all the attention she needs, I've developed a recent habit, when the babysitter comes by to watch Isabel, of collecting all of my work together and bringing it all to a nice little Chinese restaurant across the street called A Taste of China. They know me pretty well, and let me sit at one of their tables for hours while I nibble on a lunch special.

Where do you find inspiration for your writing?

Other books. The only true axiom to creative expression is that to be productive at what you do, you have to pay attention to what everyone else is doing. I think this is true for writing, for painting, for playing music, for anything that requires any sort of creative output. To put it more simply for my situation . . . if you want to write books, you have to read as many books as you can.

Which of your characters is most like you?

In *Happy Birthday, Bad Kitty*, I introduce a character named Strange Kitty. I can say without any hesitation that Strange Kitty is me as a child. I was definitely the cat who would go to a birthday party and spend the entire time sitting in the corner reading comic books rather than participating in all of the pussycat games.

When you finish a book, who reads it first?

My wife, Carina. Even if I'm on a tight deadline, she'll see it first before I even send it to my editor, Neal Porter. Carina has a fine sense of taste for the work I do. I greatly respect her opinion even when she's a little more honest than I'd like her to be.

Are you a morning person or a night owl?
Both. I suspect that I need less sleep than most people. I'm usually the first one up to make breakfast. And I'm rarely in bed before 11:00 PM. Maybe this is why I'm exhausted all the time.

What's your idea of the best meal ever?
So long as it's Chinese food, I don't care. I just love eating it. If I had to pick a favorite dish, it would be Duck Chow Fun, which I can only find in a few seedy diners in Chinatown.

Which do you like better: cats or dogs?
Oh, I know everyone is going to expect me to say cats, but in all honesty, I love them both.

What do you value most in your friends?
Sense of humor and reliability.

Where do you go for peace and quiet?
I'm the father of a one-year-old. What is this "peez kwiet" thing you speak of?

What makes you laugh out loud?
The Marx Brothers. W. C. Fields. Buster Keaton. And my daughter.

What's your favorite song?
I don't think I have one favorite song, but "If You Want to Sing Out, Sing Out" by Cat Stevens comes to mind.

Who is your favorite fictional character?
The original Captain Marvel. He's the kind of superhero designed for kids who need superheroes. SHAZAM!

What are you most afraid of?
Scorpions. ACK! They're like the creepiest parts of spiders and crabs smashed together into one nasty-looking character. Who's idea was that?

What time of year do you like best?
Spring and summer.

What's your favorite TV show?
I have to give my propers to *The Simpsons,* of course. But I'm very partial to the British mystery series *Lovejoy.*

If you were stranded on a desert island, who would you want for company?
I'm going to defy the implications of that question and say no one. As much as I'm comfortable talking for hours with any number of people, I'm also one of those people who relishes solitude. I've never had any problem with being alone for long periods of time. . . . You get a lot more work done that way.

If you could travel in time, where would you go?
America in the 1920's. All of my favorite literature, movies, and music comes from that period. I would love to have witnessed or even participated in the artistic movements of that period in history.

What's the best advice you have ever received about writing?
I had a playwriting teacher in college named Bob Butman who gave me superb advice on the subject of writer's block—it's all about PRIDE. It's a complete myth to believe that you can't think about what you want to write next because your mind is a blank. In truth, when you feel

"blocked," it's because you DO have something in mind that you want to put to paper, but you don't feel it's good enough for what you're trying to accomplish. That's the pride part. The best thing, I find, is to put it down anyways and move on. Half the challenge of the writing process is the self-editing process.

What would you do if you ever stopped writing?
I would seriously consider becoming a teacher.

What do you like best about yourself?
I have nice hands. They've always served me well.

What is your worst habit?
Biting other people's toenails.

What do you consider to be your greatest accomplishment?
Adopting our spectacular daughter, Isabel. Actually managing to get my first book (*Boing!*) published comes in second.

Where in the world do you feel most at home?
Home. I'm a homebody. I like to work at home. I like to cook at home. I like to grow my garden vegetables at home. I like being in new and different places, but I despise the process of getting there. So, because I'm not a big fan of traveling, I just like being at HOME. It's a quality about myself that runs closely with my love of solitude.

What do you wish you could do better?
I wish I was a better artist. I look at the fluidity of line and the luminous colors of paintings by such artists as Ted Lewin, Anik McGrory, Jerry Pinkney, and Arthur Rackham with complete awe.

Kitty has spent years getting used to Puppy.
Now she's got something
even more diabolical to deal with.

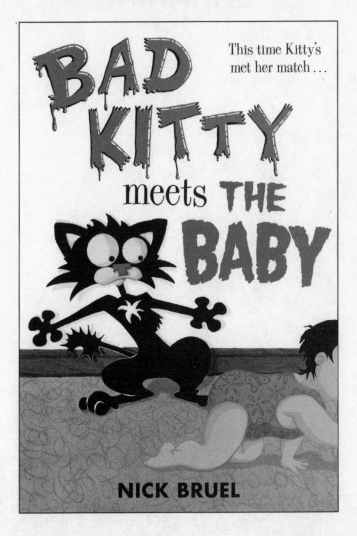

Bad Kitty's shenanigans continue in
BAD KITTY MEETS THE BABY

•INTRODUCTION•

IN THE
BEGINNING

IN THE BEGINNING, THERE WAS KITTY.

Just Kitty.

Only Kitty.

Kitty—all by herself.

And life was good.

Kitty ate her food—alone.

Kitty played with her toys—alone.

Kitty slept on the sofa—alone.

The years passed, and Kitty was happy to eat alone, play alone, and sleep alone. Life continued to be good—alone.

BUT ONE DAY . . .

. . . the skies became dark, the ground began to shake, the air became cold and dank and filled with a horrible stench.

A foul and wretched beast had arrived as if from nowhere.

Its face was deformed and grotesque. Its massive black nose was always cold and always wet. Its breath was so hot and so foul that its odor could mask the stench of a hundred dead fish lying in the sun. And it seemed to be filled with a noxious, clear liquid that continuously dripped out of the vast, gaping maw it called its mouth.

Kitty fought bravely to rid her once peaceful kingdom of the cruel beast. But even she wasn't mighty enough to defeat the evil creature.

Over time, Kitty became used to life with the beast. Even its horrible odor became tolerable. The brave Kitty had found areas of shelter where she could evade the beast and its terrible liquid.

At times, though she would never admit it, she became almost fond of the beast.

Almost.

Life was not as it once was, but eventually it became good again.

Little did Kitty know that soon there would be another.